Dear Parent:
Your child's love of reading starts here!

Every child learns to read in a different way and at his or her own speed. Some go back and forth between reading levels and read favorite books again and again. Others read through each level in order. You can help your young reader improve and become more confident by encouraging his or her own interests and abilities. From books your child reads with you to the first books he or she reads alone, there are I Can Read Books for every stage of reading:

SHARED READING
Basic language, word repetition, and whimsical illustrations, ideal for sharing with your emergent reader

BEGINNING READING
Short sentences, familiar words, and simple concepts for children eager to read on their own

READING WITH HELP
Engaging stories, longer sentences, and language play for developing readers

READING ALONE
Complex plots, challenging vocabulary, and high-interest topics for the independent reader

ADVANCED READING
Short paragraphs, chapters, and exciting themes for the perfect bridge to chapter books

I Can Read Books have introduced children to the joy of reading since 1957. Featuring award-winning authors and illustrators and a fabulous cast of beloved characters, I Can Read Books set the standard for beginning readers.

A lifetime of discovery begins with the magical words **"I Can Read!"**

Visit www.icanread.com for information
on enriching your child's reading experience.

For Barry Joel, who thinks
his grandfather is a horse

HarperCollins®, ☷®, and I Can Read Book® are trademarks of HarperCollins Publishers.

Manufactured in China. For information address HarperCollins Children's Books, a division of HarperCollins Publishers, 10 East 53rd Street, New York, NY 10022. www.harpercollinschildrens.com

Library of Congress Cataloging-in-Publication Data

Hoff, Syd.
   The horse in Harry's room / story and pictures by Syd Hoff.
     p.   cm.—(An I can read book)
   Summary: Although no one else can see it, Harry is very pleased to have a horse in his room.
   ISBN-10: 0-06-029426-4 (trade bdg.) — ISBN-13: 978-0-06-029426-7 (trade bdg.)
   ISBN-10: 0-06-022483-5 (lib. bdg.) — ISBN-13: 978-0-06-022483-7 (lib. bdg.)
   ISBN-10: 0-06-444073-7 (pbk.) — ISBN-13: 978-0-06-444073-8 (pbk.)
   [1. Imaginary playmates—Fiction.] I. Title. II. Series.
PZ7.H672Ho 2001   00-39716
[E]—dc21   CIP
                                                   AC

12 13 SCP 40 39 38 37 36 35
❖

BEGINNING
1
READING

The Horse in Harry's Room

story and pictures by
Syd Hoff

HarperCollins*Publishers*

Harry had a horse in his room.

Nobody knew.

He could ride him in a circle
without knocking over
the chair or the dresser.

He could jump him over the bed

without hitting his head

on the ceiling.

"Oh, it's great to have a horse,"
said Harry.
"I hope I will always have him.
I hope he will always stay."

His mother looked into Harry's room
to see what he was doing.
She did not see the horse.

9

His father looked into Harry's room
to see what he was doing.
He did not see the horse.

"Giddyap," they heard him say

when he wanted his horse to go.

"Whoa," they heard him say
when he wanted his horse to stop.

But they did not see

a horse in Harry's room.

"Let's take Harry to the country,"
said Father.
"Let's show him some real horses."

Harry did not care if he ever
went to the country.
He had his own horse in his room!

Every night
when Harry went to sleep,
he knew his horse would stay
and watch over him.

Every day
when Harry went to school,
he knew his horse would wait
for him to come home.

One day the teacher said,

"Let us all tell about something today."

One girl told about a dress

she wore to a party.

One boy told about a glove

he used for baseball.

"I have a horse in my room,"
said Harry.
"I can ride him in a circle
without knocking over
the chair or the dresser.
I can jump him over the bed
without hitting my head
on the ceiling."
The children laughed.
"Sometimes thinking about a thing
is the same as having it,"
said the teacher.

It was Sunday.

Harry's mother and father

took him for a drive.

They rode out of the city,

far out into the country.

Harry saw cows and chickens
and green grass.
And he saw HORSES!
"Look at the horses, Harry,"
said Mother.

Harry saw horses running.

Harry saw horses kicking.

Harry saw horses nibbling.

"Horses should always be free
to run and kick and nibble,"
said Father.

When they got home,

Harry ran right to his room.

"Horses should always be free
to run and kick and nibble,"
Harry said to his horse.
"If you want to go,
you may go."

Harry's horse looked to the right.

Harry's horse looked to the left.

Then he stayed right where he was.

"Oh, I'm glad," said Harry.

And he knew he would have his horse

as long as he wanted him.